To my kids, always remember:
You can be anything you want in this life.
Just don't be a Democrat.
--Love Dad

CHAPTER 1

The spaceship touched down.

Inside, Hozay glanced at the eleven other aliens in the craft, each one strapped into their seat, sitting motionless, staring blankly ahead in the trance-like state that defined their existence. Sometimes he envied them—not having the desire, or ability, to think for himself would certainly make life less complicated.

When the hydraulics of an overhead hatch hissed and a metal ramp fell gently to the floor, he quickly snapped his head back and faked an expressionless forward gaze, letting his mouth hang lazily open so that he would look just as dopey as the others.

The group's leader descended the ramp and opened a door to the outside. He looked around the room at his followers, fully pleased at their subservience. Then, he sent them a mind-control command: find food.

In an obedient synchronized fashion, the aliens unstrapped themselves and exited the ship in single file.

Hozay mixed into the middle of the line and, as always, mimicked the others movement for movement--lest the leader realize that he had a mind of his own and the ability to think, giving him the potential to stray from the herd. Of course, he did have a mind and he did have that potential, but he had yet to find the planet that was worth the risk of defecting.

As they stepped out onto the moonlit ground in the middle of a clearing in the woods, each of the aliens wandered away from the ship in a different direction. Hozay took in the sensations of this new world--the smell of various flowers and leaves, the feel of tree bark, and the sound of crickets and other late night critters. This place did not seem very different from so many others they had landed on.

But maybe, he hoped, it *was* different.

He looked around and, sure that no eyes were on him, gazed toward the heavens. With a deep sigh, he prayed. In his mind. No words. No gestures or movements. No indication of any kind as to what he was doing. He asked God, as he had so many times before, to let this be the place he could finally call home.

A bustling in the green brush at his feet grabbed his attention.

He kneeled and listened carefully. Something was down there, scurrying in the leaves. His eyes darted left and right, searching for the source of the sound. The alien shot his hand into the brush and snatched a brown rat. He stood and held the squirming animal up to the moonlight to study it. It was small, but that meant nothing. Sometimes, small things had delicious brains. He put the rat's head to his nose and breathed in.

The putrid odor burned his nostrils and flowed down the back of his throat where it settled like a noxious mix of infected cosmic dust. He gagged and coughed, and then slammed the little animal to the ground. For good measure, he stomped on it.

"Look!" a fellow alien said, pointing through a thicket of small trees at a dim light that shined in the distance.

Hozay joined the others and ventured through the woods toward the light up to a small campsite. As they neared a cluster of tents, a sweet smell permeated the still air. The aliens all stopped to take a few deep breaths, grunting and groaning with satisfaction at the delightful aroma. Then, each alien found a tent to enter.

But Hozay paused. He took another deep inhale, savoring the scent that tantalized his nose. It was unlike anything he had ever smelled before. This place *was* different.

A moment later, screams from a nearby tent flooded the night air, but they were quickly muffled and the night turned silent again. A groan of pain came from another tent but that also quickly faded to back silence. From another tent, the sound of a scuffle, but it lasted only a second, ending with a bone-shattering crack and a whimper.

A man with a shotgun burst out of the tent that Hozay stood in front of. "Who the hell are you?" he said, raising his weapon and pointing it at the alien's chest. He squinted to get a better look at the being that stood before him in the night. As similar as the alien looked to a human, it was clear to the man that it was not from his world. He pulled the trigger.

The shot rang out and a spray of lead peppered Hozay's chest. Unaffected, the alien ignored it.

A look of horror overcame the man. He stepped backward, tripping and stumbling onto the ground in his tent.

Hozay followed. He reached down and grabbed the sides of the man's head, pulling him up and taking a giant sniff into his ear. The alien's mouth watered.

As the man struggled to no avail, Hozay put his mouth to the side of his victim's head and sucked. Brain shot through the human's ear like a lumpy smoothie through a thin straw. When the alien finished slurping, he dropped the lifeless body and kneeled beside it.

He dug his fingers into his victim's facial orifices, struggling to reach deeper into the human's skull and scrape up every last bit of brain. As he sucked his fingers clean from the most delectable meal in a hundred thousand light years, another thought command came from his leader: bring food.

Before returning to the ship, Hozay closed his eyes and savored the wondrous taste that lingered in his mouth. Silently, he again asked God to let this finally be the place he can call home. Then, he started back toward the ship with the others.

The now brainless human victims stumbled out of their tents and followed.

***

President Dudley Toobit stood behind the ball and lined up his shot--a 150-yard carry over a water hazard and onto a forgiving fairway.

The slight breeze coming from the rear had a little bite to it, not yet warmed by the sun that still lay halfway below the horizon. Even though it was early, this was the best time to play. The only time, in fact, to play alone and without interruptions. This was something he had learned over the course of his first term, which was coming to an end in the next couple of months.

He held out his hand and snapped his fingers. "Three wood."

His caddy produced the club, and the president took it into his grip and stood over the ball. He spoke softly, to himself, repeating the words of the golf pros that he worked with on a daily basis. "Front shoulder down, hands in, back leg straight." He eased the club head back until it reached the top of his backswing, waiting just a moment at this highest point, and then--

His cell phone's ring cut through the morning air.

"Jesus!" He slammed his club on the ground repeatedly, cracking the graphite shaft, and then tossed it into the rough.

As his caddy hurried to retrieve the broken club, the president checked his caller id: John Hatchet-Secretary of Defense.

It should have read: John Hatchet, jerk-off, if I didn't need a token Republican in my cabinet I would never have to deal with you, you goddam asshole.

But it didn't. It read: John Hatchet-Secretary of Defense.

"What do you want, Hatchet?" the president said.

"There's an emergency, Mr. President."

"There's always an emergency somewhere. What is it?"

"Aliens."

The president shook his head in disgust. Everything was an emergency to this racist pig if the people involved had skin darker than a marshmallow. He spoke loud and slow, mocking a mentally retarded person. "I'm legalizing them." Then, in the angry voice he used for Hatchet or any other Republican, snarled, "Get over it."

"Not those kinds of aliens, sir."

"Oh, what kind, then? White ones? Colonizers? I doubt you'd be calling about them."

"Real aliens. From space."

"Space aliens? Is this some kind of joke?"

"I wish it were, sir. And it gets worse. They're also zombies."

After letting the words sink in, the president stared ahead, deep in thought, completely and utterly unsure of what to do next--"a hundred fifty yards," he muttered, disappointed that he no longer had his three wood for the shot.

***

The president kept the meeting to a small group of his most trusted advisors. Only his campaign manager, press secretary and caddy were present--and General Hatchet, since he already knew what was going on.

As they watched a video of brain-eating aliens on the screen at the front of the Situation Room, the president spoke. "So, we know what we're dealing with," he said. "The question is *how* do we deal with them?"

"Seal the area and obliterate it," said Veronica Jacket, his campaign manager. "It's our only choice."

"Obliterate it? What about collateral damage?" Hatchet asked.

"What about it?" Jacket snapped. "We can't tippy-toe around this. We stop this immediately or it gets out of hand. Right now they're contained in a bible-thumping little skidmark of a hillbilly town that nobody gives half a crap about. We have to strike. Now."

"You're talking about an entire town of innocent people," Hatchet said. "Our military's got the greatest technology and expertise in the world. We can be more surgical than this. We can spare tens of thousands of lives. We can--"

"If we're going to blow up an entire town," the president said, "then we'll need a cover." He turned to Press Secretary Bob Bard. "We'll say there was an explosion of some kind. Find out what's close enough to use--a gas station, a factory, whatever. Blow it up yourself if you have to. But make it look really real."

"And get this video deleted immediately," Jacket demanded. "We don't need people getting all crazy because of some internet video. In fact, monitor all internet and phone usage from that town. Nothing gets out about this."

"I'll call our people in the media," Bard said, stepping away from the table with his cell phone in hand.

The president leaned back in his chair and clasped his hands behind his head as he thought about the plan. Yeah, keeping things hush-hush was always a safe bet. What people don't know can't hurt them. Well, it can, but it's usually too late by the time it does. And that's just as good. Still, he hated seeing a crisis go to waste. "Is there any way we can use this to our advantage?" he asked Jacket. "The election's only six months away. Maybe we can use this to make me look even better."

"I don't think so. Sure, if you save the day you're a hero. But then we're also letting everyone know about the collateral damage. This is a classic case of 'what they don't know won't hurt them.'"

The president's face lit up. "That's exactly what I was thinking," he said with a beaming smile.

"A situation like this is like playing with fire," Jacket said. "If anything goes wrong, we get burnt. You're way up in the polls. Let's just play it safe."

"Christ," Hatchet said. "Don't you ever stop campaigning?"

The president glared at the Republican. Boy, wouldn't it be nice if these space zombies ate *him*. "Just kill the damn aliens. Spare your precious bible-thumpers if you have to—I don't really care."

Hatchet returned a cold stare, then stood and started to the door.

"Hold it!" Bard called. "Hatchet, wait!"

Bard started a video on his cell phone and held it out for all to see. As in the footage they had watched earlier, a zombie pulled its victim close and sniffed the human head. But this time, instead of sucking the human's brain out, the creature wretched and gagged, dropped the human, and lost interest.

"It turns out there's a pattern here," Bard said. "Every person that has been let go has been a Democrat."

Jacket leaned in. "Are you saying ..."

Bard nodded. "They only eat Republicans."

"Let me get this straight," Toobit said. "They only eat Republicans, turning them into zombies who, in turn, eat more Republicans?"

Bard nodded. The room remained silent for a moment as the president and Jacket shared a look. They smiled and high-fived. Then, the president let out a high-pitched whoop and hugged his caddy.

"We'll change the demographics of the country," Jacket said through a giddy giggle.

"We'll never lose another election," Toobit cheered.

"We'll never leave the White House," they screamed together as they embraced and jumped up and down.

"Oh no you don't," Hatchet said. "I'm going to take care of these aliens. There'll be nothing left of them when I'm done."

"Sorry, Hatchet," the president said. "Plans have changed."

"What do you mean? How have they changed?"

"You're not bombing anything or anyone."

"You're going to just sit there while zombies from space kill millions of people just because they oppose you politically?"

The president meandered to the corner of the room and pulled a seven iron from his golf bag. He carefully wrapped his fingers around the grip. "I will certainly not just sit there while zombies from space kill millions of people that oppose me politically." He took a slow-motion practice swing. "But I might play a few rounds while it happens," he said with a smile.

Hatchet marched up to Toobit and waved his finger in the president's face. "You're out of your mind if you think I'm going to let you get away with this."

Toobit looked to Jacket and gave a slight nod. A moment later, a half-dozen Secret Service agents rushed the room and manhandled a struggling Hatchet to the floor and cuffed him.

"The American people aren't going to stand for this," he called as he was dragged out of the room by his ankles.

"Done deal," Bard said as he stepped over the Secretary of Defense and re-entered the room. "Major networks, newspapers, and social media are going to black out everything."

"Perfect," Jacket said. "By the time anyone figures out what's going on, Republicans will be extinct."

But even with a media blackout, there was one thing that didn't sit right with the president. "We have a blackout on newspapers, T.V., and the internet, but what about talk radio?"

"I wouldn't worry," Jacket said. "The rest of the media will neutralize them."

But the president wasn't convinced. "Even you-know-who?"

CHAPTER 2

"With brilliance borrowed from God." Flash Lambo let his thunderous trademark slogan linger in the air a moment before continuing the introduction of his radio broadcast. "Welcome to the most intelligent and educational entertainment anywhere across the fruited plains." He grabbed the microphone and walked over to the window.

Five stories below the radio studio, the street was jam-packed with conservative protestors. At the far end of the crowd, a large banner read "Protect Our Borders." Dozens of handheld signs, inscribed with a similar sentiment, waved in the sea of patriots. A roar came from the crowd as they noticed their favorite broadcaster looking down.

Flash waved. "It's great to see you down there, my friends," he said into the microphone. "I'll be talking to some of you throughout the show. Hopefully, I'll have time to join you down there as well."

Another roar erupted.

Flash returned to his seat and set the microphone on the desk. "Well, the phones are already lit up like a Christmas tree. Can I refer to a Christmas tree or will a Democrat head explode somewhere? In any case, let's go to line one. Bill from Falls Church, Virginia. Bill, how are you today?"

"Not bad, Flash. I'm a first time caller, so I'm a bit nervous, but I just want to get your take on the alien spaceship. Is the government behind this?"

Flash chuckled. "Alright, so we're starting off with a bang today. Did you say alien spaceship?"

"Yes, sir. I heard some people talking early this morning at the coffee shop, but there's nothing on the news or anything."

Flash slapped the large neat stack of printouts that sat in the corner of his desk. "Well, I don't have anything about aliens in my pile of papers."

"This might sound crazy but, if it's true, do you think maybe the president is one of them? An alien, I mean."

"Well, Bill, he may as well be from another planet. I mean, let's face it, he is about as far from an American as you can get and, in so many ways, seems to be almost inhuman. He is certainly *inhumane*. All we need to do is look at the atrocities he is allowing to happen all over the globe as he tees off at a new golf course every weekend. So, I guess you could say, if a president wanted to throw the entire planet into chaos, as an alien visitor might want to do, this president's policies would do just that. They *are* doing that. Thanks for the call, Bill.

"Ok, line two. Another local call. Janet, from Lyon Village."

"Hi, Flash. Count me as a proud Earther, too. That man is not from this planet. But, what I heard is that these aliens are zombies? Brain-eating zombies. Is that a thing? Alien zombies?"

Flash chuckled. "Ah, an Earther. Alien zombies. Well, I have as good a sense of humor as anyone in broadcasting, so I do appreciate these calls, and I will actually address this issue.

"Let's say that there are aliens on this planet and that they are looking to eat our brains. What would happen? Well, there would be a movement, from the left of course, that would say, essentially: don't they have the right to eat what they want? Who are we to stop them from eating our brains--provided of course they don't wash the brains down with a large sugary soda.

"So, if you come across any zombie aliens, you should allow them to eat your brain. I mean it. It's the American thing to do. We are obligated to make that sacrifice.

"In fact, as someone who is always looking to promote American values, I would like to offer my own brain to our intergalactic friends. Yes, my brain, infused with brilliance from God--"

With a click, the microphone went dead. Flash tapped the end and blew into it. "Sneadle," he yelled to his long-time producer. "What's going on?" Perfect timing for a technical malfunction--right in the middle of a brilliant monolog.

"Sneadle," he called again as he repeatedly tapped the mic. He walked to the producer's room in the back of the studio and pushed open the door. "Sneadle, what's going--"

Flash's knees buckled when he saw his producer, kneeling in the center of the room, his cranium cracked open like a jack-o-lantern. Standing behind him, a human-like creature had his face buried in the man's head, sucking and slurping like the grand-prize winner at a county fair pie-eating contest.

Flash stumbled backwards into his room, tripping over the desk and pulling everything on it to the floor as he tried, unsuccessfully, to avoid falling to the ground.

The clatter caught the attention of the alien and the victim. As the alien kneeled to lick the fallen brain scraps off the floor, Sneadle—now a brainless human--started toward Flash.

Flash tried to scramble to his feet, but Sneadle grabbed him with a hand on each side of the head. The zombie pulled his victim up, face to face, his drooling mouth opened wide.

Flash braced his hands against Sneadle's chest, pushing back hard to keep the zombie's mouth at bay. But Sneadle was freakishly strong, and his mouth inched closer.

Flash stared into his producer's eyes. The dyed-in-the-wool conservative that he had known for years had a look in his eyes that was ... different. It was a look that said more than just "I'm going to eat your brain." It said "I deserve this. You owe me this. How dare you stop me from taking what I want."

It was the look of a Democrat.

Flash averted his eyes. If he was going to die, there was no way he wanted a Democrat--and he knew by instinct that's exactly what this creature was--to be the last thing he saw.

15

He spotted his microphone on the floor and reached down, struggling to extend his arm enough to get his fingertips on it.

The creature pressed its mouth against Flash's ear and sucked.

Vacuum pressure built up in Flash's head. The pain was excruciating, the slurping sound in his ear, deafening.

As he stretched harder for the microphone, the tip of his middle finger grazed it and he pulled it closer. He reached again and finally wrapped his fingers around it, squeezed it tight, and then swung it at Sneadle's head.

It struck with a thud and the zombie's grip weakened.

Flash pulled himself free and swung again, landing another solid blow to the head.

Sneadle grunted, but moved forward, arms outstretched to recapture his victim. There was only one door out of the room and the zombie had it blocked.

Flash lowered his shoulder and plowed into the brain-eater. They crashed through the door and tumbled across the floor until they slammed into the far wall.

Flash untangled himself from the zombie and raced down a nearby flight of stairs to the safety of the street.

***

What minutes ago was a peaceful conservative rally on a quiet street now looked like the zombie version of an old-time saloon brawl.

Flash pushed his way through the mayhem as, all around him, victims succumbed to the brain-sucking of the zombies. He continued pushing his way through the dense crowd until he came face to face with a zombie, his path blocked by the drooling brain eater.

"Lambo," a man shouted, and tossed him a two-foot length of metal pipe.

In one fell swoop, Flash caught the pipe and swung it into the head of the creature that stood before him.

A crack rang out as the side of the zombie's head caved in. The zombie stumbled, but quickly regained his footing, and then lunged forward.

As Flash loaded up for another swing, he was grabbed from behind and pulled backwards by his shirt collar. He struggled to turn, but lost his footing and was dragged through the crowd, around the corner, and behind a brick building.

The instant he was released, he jumped to his feet, turned, and took a mighty swing.

The pipe stopped dead as if it hit a brick wall, caught in his assailant's powerful hand. As Flash struggled to pull his weapon free, he realized that the creature standing in front of him wasn't a zombie, but a human. A massive human--easily six and a half feet tall and probably three hundred pounds of solid muscle. Next to this huge man was a woman of average size.

"I'm Guy," the man said, letting go of the pipe and straightening the collar of Flash's shirt that he had used as a handle. "Sorry to be so rough, Flash, but it looked like you needed some help out there."

"I'm Maria," the woman said with an extremely heavy Hispanic accent. "Maria Consuela Conchita Gonzales." She peeked around the corner, checking on the zombie battleground.

Flash poked his head around the corner also. The zombies were wandering the area, searching for scraps of brain that had fallen to the ground or picking them off each other's shirts like monkey's cleaning each other at the zoo. Only a couple of non-zombies remained, but they didn't last long, quickly swarmed by the horde of brain eaters.

Flash's phone rang and General Hatchet's name flashed on caller id.

"General, what's going on? The streets are crawling with zombies."

The General spoke fast. "Listen. I don't have much time. A small group of space zombies landed on Earth this morning. Everyone they eat turns into a zombie. But they only attack Republicans. And the Toobit administration is going to let them roam free."

"What do you mean let them roam free?"

"It fits their agenda. It's an opportunity to--"

"Exterminate the opposition."

"Exactly. And they've blacked out all media, social media, everything."

"What about the military?"

"Forget the military. I've been detained for disagreeing so you can be sure they'll put some lackey in charge. Flash, you can reach more Republicans in a shorter time than anyone. You're the only one that can save the country."

"But General--"

A sucking sound, like a whirlpool draining down a kitchen sink, echoed through the phone.

Flash pulled the phone from his ear and cringed. "Space zombies," he said to Guy and Maria. "They only attack Republicans and the administration is going to sit around and let it happen."

"Wait," Maria said. "These things, they only are eating Republicans?" She paused with a curious look on her face. "This is interesting, no? No bueno. But interesting, yes? Si?"

"I don't know," Flash said. He wasn't really listening, and was instead deep in thought about what he saw when he had looked in Sneadle's eyes--the look of a Democrat. At first, he couldn't understand it, but now it made sense-- take away a Republican's brain and you're left with a Democrat. With no help from the military, he knew it wouldn't be long before these zombie Democrats sucked every Republican brain in the country.

"We need to find a way to get the truth out and let the country know what's going on."

Guy smiled and pounded his fist into his hand. "You guys are safe here, so I'm getting back out there." He started toward the zombies.

Flash grabbed the big man's shoulder. "We'll never win."

"You gonna let these space zombie things win?"

"No. We're going to use our brains. Fortunately, God gave me a big one. We're gonna let people know what's going on. This way, we can organize. Strength in numbers. We can't fight them alone. We need to build an army of Republicans."

"Si. Smart," Maria said, pointing to Flash. "Very smart. You need to get on the radio. Come on, let's get to your studio." She started back toward the zombies.

Flash grabbed her shoulder. "Are you crazy? The place is crawling with zombies. If these things are only eating Republicans, we need to stay in Democrat areas.

"But you need the studio to broadcast," Maria said.

"I know another place in a much safer location."

***

Flash led Guy and Maria through the seedy downtown streets where pimps, hobos, and drug dealers populated every corner. Maria nervously looked back over her shoulder just about every other step and even Guy, the largest and most physically intimidating man Flash had ever seen in person, appeared more than a little unsettled. "Do we really need to be here?" he asked.

"Yes," Flash said. "If these zombies are only eating Republicans, then we need to stay in a Democrat area."

A scream came from the distance. Further up the block, a street thug in an oversized hoodie jumped in front of a female pedestrian. He ripped the woman's pocketbook from her shoulder, then stole a nearby bicycle that was lying on the ground and rode away. At the next corner, he was kicked off the bike by another thug who took the pocketbook and then sprinted in the other direction. As he lay on the ground, a child escaped from the local elementary school by hopping the playground's chain-link fence. He flicked his cigarette at the man on the ground, grabbed the bike, and raced down the street.

"Definitely a Democrat area," Guy said. "I think we'll be safe from the zombies here."

When they finally arrived at an abandoned building on the far side of town, Flash cupped his hands up against the window to get a view inside. It was difficult to peruse the unlit space through the dirty, grimy windows but, on a table in the rear of the room, he saw what he was hoping to find--a microphone. As he rattled the locked door handle, Guy read the small sign above the building's entrance: American Airwaves. "What's that?" He asked.

"American Airwaves was a liberal talk radio station," Flash said. "It failed after a couple of months." He jiggled the locked door handle again. "But they'll have all the equipment I need to broadcast if we can get in."

"Broadcast?" Guy said. "Come on. We gotta get out there and fight. That's what everyone else will be doing."

"No. We need to alert the country and let everyone know what's going on. We need to organize."

Guy scoffed. "You're gonna hide behind a microphone? Let's kick some alien zombie ass."

"There's no way we'd win. Remember, we won't be getting any help from the government. Not the feds, not locals. Nothing. In fact, you can bet they'll be working against us."

"Who needs them?" Guy looked around, as if there was someone around that might hear, and spoke in a low voice. "I have more firepower than you can even imagine. Guns, grenades, rocket launchers, you name it."

Flashes eyes widened. "Grenades? Rocket launchers?"

"Let's just say I'm not a 'wait around for someone to save me' kind of guy. It's all about being prepared."

"No," Maria said. "Flash is right. We must spread the word. Later, there will be plenty of time for fighting."

Guy looked back and forth between Flash and Maria a few times. "Plenty of time for fighting? You promise?"

"You can count on it," Flash said.

"I don't know," Guy said, "I'm not too good at standing around doing nothing."

"It's not nothing," Flash insisted. "We're being smart. We have one advantage and we need to use it." He tapped his forefinger on the side of his head. "Up here. Our brains."

"Got news for ya," Guy said. "Unless you can put some poison in your brain and spoon feed it to them, I think even your brilliant brain from God is gonna be useless." He slammed his fist into an open palm.

"Sometimes a good old-fashioned knuckle sandwich is the best way to solve a problem."

"Trust me on this." Flash jiggled the door knob again. He pushed the door, but it didn't budge.

Guy gently brushed Flash aside. He sized up the door, took two steps back and then lowered his shoulder and barreled his giant frame forward. The frame split with a crack as the door flew open. He pulled the door from the few splinters of wood that still held it on and tossed it to the side. "See? Muscle always wins."

"Glad you're on my side," Flash said as he slid past the big man and into the building.

Once inside, he headed straight for the control room and flipped on all the power switches. "You guys man the windows and doors. Keep lookout. There's no telling how long we have before the zombies make their way around here."

Guy stood in the open doorway, arms crossed, and Maria stationed herself by the rear windows.

"Let's see what we got," Flash said to himself as he sat down at the table with the microphone. He flipped the switch and tapped the mic with his finger.

"With brilliance borrowed from God," he bellowed into the mic. "This is Flash Lambo with an important message. Brain-eating aliens have landed and are turning Republicans into Democrat zombies. If you are a Republican, a conservative, you are in danger." He placed his cell phone on the table and gave out the number. The phone rang immediately. He put it on speaker and kept it

23

close the microphone. "Ok, we have someone on the line, who do we have?"

An old curmudgeonly voice answered. "I call bull. The president just gave a speech on the T.V. and he says there ain't no aliens but that even if there was aliens, that they're friendly aliens."

"You can't possibly believe that," Flash said. "It doesn't even make any sense."

"Well, why should we care if anyone eats your brains, anyway? Your supposed Republican brains ain't done nothing but cause problems in this country for forever."

"Ok, not what I was hoping for." Flash hung up and immediately the phone rang again. "Yeah, like that other caller said. I don't really give a--"

Flash disconnected again.

"See?" Guy called from inside the door frame. "We're wasting our time."

"Only Democrats are tuned in to this station," Flash realized. "I'm going up on the roof to see if we can transmit on a different frequency. We need to reach a different audience." He scanned the room for something he could use to change the station's transmitting frequency and found a roll of packing tape on a shelf in the corner. He could use it for an old trick he remembered from his early days as a techie.

On the roof, he found the transmitter--a galvanized metal case with two power leads in and two antennae leads out. Inside sat the crystal oscillator that determined the transmission frequency. He opened the case and wrapped the top half of the crystal in packing tape. It had been years since he worked on the technical side of radio, but he knew this would be enough to change the frequency-- and the radio station where his voice could be heard.

Once downstairs again, he got back behind the mic and started as he always did. "With brilliance borrowed from God." But there was no power.

Images of Sneadle the zombie flashed in his mind as he remembered the last time his mic lost power. He looked around nervously. "You guys ok? You see anything out there?"

Guy and Maria confirmed that all was fine at their lookout posts.

Flash tapped his mic and blew into it. Nothing. As he began to deduce the source of the problem, he noticed a frayed wire under the table. The wire that led to the microphone had been ripped from the wall.

Flash's blood boiled. He grabbed the frayed ends of wire and stepped up to Guy, nose to nose. "What the hell is wrong with you?" he yelled, waving the loose wires in front of the big man's face.

"I don't know what you're talking about," Guy said. He looked at the wire and shrugged. "But I guess talking is out. Time to fight?"

"If we're going to stand any chance," Flash scolded, "there are millions of people that we need to reach, first."

"How long you gonna hide in here and protect your precious brain, anyway?"

25

"You wanna go fight?" Flash gestured to open doorway. "Be my guest."

As the two men argued, a small commotion across the street caught their attention. A man and a handful of women--loud, raucous, and seemingly intoxicated--made their way from a black limousine into the building on the corner which was marked by a flickering red neon "Motel" sign.

"Hey, I know him," Guy said, pointing across the street. "Didn't that guy used to be president."

It was former President Mo Lester. Better known by most as the Philanderer-in-Chief. When Flash realized who it was, his mind raced. This might be a good break. If he could make Lester understand the seriousness of the situation, maybe he could convince the charismatic elder statesman to rally the Democrats.

CHAPTER 3

Loud music and boisterous laughter emanated from the motel room.

Flash pounded on the door until the sounds inside the room quieted and the door opened slightly. President Lester popped his head out--a bra dangling from his ear and a martini glass, filled to the rim, in his hand. "I did not have sexual relations with that space zombie."

"What?" Flash said.

Lester unhooked the bra from his ear. "Oh, uh nothing. Flash, is that you? What are you doing here? A little exposé?"

"No, Mr. President, I--"

"Cause you know, I never mind a little expose, ay?" He threw his head back and laughed hard. His drink spilled over the rim of the glass and he slurped up the drip from the bottom of it.

"Mr. President. You know about the space zombies."

Lester stopped laughing and tried, unsuccessfully, to force a serious look on his face. "I'm sorry, Flash, I don't know what you're talking about," he said, with a chuckle.

"Oh, come on. You mentioned them right when you opened the door. I never said a word about them. It's obvious that you know."

"Well, that depends on what the meaning of 'know' is." A sly grin snuck its way onto his face. "Sometimes 'no' means 'yes.'" He threw his head back in laughter again.

"Not that 'no.' K-N-O-W."

"I'm going to have to stick with my original story. I don't *know* what you're talking about."

"Mr. President, the zombies are eating every Republican brain in sight. I know you don't care too much about that, with them being Republicans and all, but here's the thing--if this president gets rid of all the Republicans, he'll be in office forever. Forever. That means you'll never get your chance to get back in the White House."

Lester suddenly looked legitimately concerned. "I did have fun in that house," he said before pausing in thought and smiling. "A lot of fun."

"So you'll help?"

"No. Truth is, I'm having way more fun since I left the White House. No media, no reporters. Besides, I party there all the time, anyway." He looked left and right, making sure no one was around to hear him. "Truth is, Toobit couldn't tie his shoes without me, politically speaking. I advise him on everything. In return, every day's a party for me. Heck, I think I enjoy the Toobit presidency more than my own. All the fun, none of the hassle."

From inside the room, a woman's hand gently rested on Lester's shoulder.

Lester turned. "Be patient, babe. I'll be right there."

The door opened a little wider and the woman came forward and stepped into the doorway. She put her arm around the ex-president, kissed him on the cheek, and then took a drag of a cigar.

Through the puff of thick smoke, a curious, confused look came to her face. She dropped the cigar and stepped on it, then cleared the smoky air with her hand and studied Flash curiously. She sniffed. Her eyes widened with that crazy Democrat look and she lunged forward, reaching for Flash's head.

Flash immediately realized this wasn't simply a typical Democrat floozy, but a zombie. He jumped back to avoid her clutch but stumbled and fell to the ground.

The zombie plowed past Lester and reached down, grabbing Flash by the sides of his head. Her grip was tight as she lifted her prey off the ground.

Flash flailed and punched. His fists landed solid blows on the zombie's body, but the creature was undeterred.

Guy stepped in, trying to pull Flash free from the zombie's grip, but a half-dozen more female zombies bounded from the room and, in flying leaps, created a pile-on with Flash, Guy, and Maria at the bottom.

"Cover your heads," Flash called from the bottom of the heap of bodies. He could feel and hear the zombies sucking desperately all around his head and neck, looking for a way to get to his brain.

Then, suddenly, they stopped.

The zombies dismounted the pile and stepped away. They now ignored the humans, and seemed to be listening to something. Mesmerized, they walked, with purpose, down the street.

"Where are they going?" Guy asked.

"I don't know," Flash said. "But we're following. Something's controlling them and we need to find out what it is."

***

Flash, Guy, and Maria trailed the zombies through the streets, across town, and deep into the woods. When they finally stopped, they hid behind a row of bushes, looking down over a clearing which was nuzzled between the base of the small hills that surrounded it. An alien spaceship sat in the center of the clearing.

In front of the ship, a single alien--apparently the leader--sat at a table. Hundreds of zombies, in a single-file line that stretched through the woods, approached the table one by one. Each stopped, stepped up to the table, and vomited on it.

As the leader dug his hands into the overflowing vile pile of semi-digested brain mush and shoveled it into his mouth, the zombie followers headed back toward the city in search of more brains.

"Interesting," Maria said with a voice full of amazement. "Never have I seen something like this."

"Shh," Flash said. "If they hear us, it'll be *our* brains on that table."

"You wouldn't want that," Guy said sarcastically, still annoyed at that he was not yet fighting. "Your brain is too important to be on the table with anyone else's. Maybe you should have a special table just for you with a sign that says, 'Greatest Brain in the World.'"

Flash ignored the insult, instead focusing on the line of aliens. "Amazing," he said with fascination.

"Amazing?" Guy said. "Zombies vomit brains into a pile and you think it's amazing?"

Entranced, Flash kept his eyes on the zombies. "They're so incredibly advanced."

"Advanced? They're brain eating, brain vomiting, brainless slobbering zombies."

"Exactly. These aliens have probably evolved for millions of years to become exactly that." He faced Guy to explain. "Like a cockroach. They're filthy, disgusting insects and every chance you get to step on one and squash it, you do. But they can survive a nuclear blast. They've evolved for millions of years to become a revolting, grotesque insect designed to do only one thing--survive.

"These aliens are the same way. They've evolved to become the universe's most perfect socialist being. They exist for one reason only--to serve their leader. And the brainless zombies that they create follow along like ... brainless zombies.

"Remember when the zombies were about to eat us and they just stopped in their tracks and came here? Think about it. Why would zombies pass up brains?"

"Because their master told them too?"

"Exactly."

Guy looked at the line of zombies in the distance, which seemed to be growing longer by the second. "Well, that's great. We've made the discovery. We understand them. Now what do we do?"

"You really have as much firepower as you said?" Flash asked.

"Yeah. But there's hundreds of them now, if not thousands. *Now* you want to fight?"

"We only need to take care of the leader."

"Why just the leader?" Guy asked.

"What happens when you take a leader away from socialists?"

"Useful idiots become useless idiots?"

"Right," Flash said. "Take away their leader, and I bet that these things won't be able to survive on their own."

"Loco," Maria said. "Loco, loco, loco. You think that killing the leader will magically just get rid of all these other zombies? It can't possibly work. No. No, no, no."

"It'll work," Flash said. "Don't doubt me. I know them better than they know themselves."

"I don't know," Maria said, her Hispanic accent getting stronger as she grew nervous. "Maybe we try to broadcast again. I like that idea better. Si?"

"No," Guy said with a look of satisfaction. "Let's get my weapons."

***

Tables and shelves, full of weapons and survival equipment, lined every wall of the concrete basement bunker. Flash eyed a slew of guns and grenades sitting on a table in the corner. He picked up a Glock to get a feel for the cold heavy steel in his hands and wondered if it would be enough to take out the alien zombie leader?

Guy tossed a duffel bag at Flash's feet in front of a standing metal cabinet. "Load up. Who knows what the next few days will bring."

Flash opened the cabinet and poured through its contents, tossing anything he thought might come in handy into the bag: batteries, rolls of wire, bags of vacuum-packed food, canteens. He looked around, still amazed at the weapons that filled the room. "It's like a military depot in here," he said as he continued stuffing items into the duffel bag.

"Let's just say I don't like playing 'damsel in distress,'"Guy said. He grabbed a large black metal case from a shelf and set it on the table in front of him. He flipped the lid and pulled out a Bazooka, held it at arm's length, and admired it. "Say hello to my little friend," he said quietly, to himself, before securing it back in its case.

Flash continued searching through the cabinet until Maria spoke behind him--strangely, without her Hispanic accent. "Both of you, drop everything and put your hands up real slow."

Flash turned to find himself staring into the end of a double barrel shotgun. "Quit playing around. Save it for the zombies." He put his hand on the barrel of the gun to push it away from his face, but Maria pushed back, keeping it square between his eyes.

"Does it look like I'm playing?" she said. "Get your hands up."

Both men put their hands in the air and Maria nodded to two pair of handcuffs hanging on the side of a table. "Put those on. Both of you. One side on your wrist, the other on the leg of that table."

"What is this about?" Flash asked as he and Guy fitted the cuffs on themselves.

"I just can't let you do it," Maria said.

"Can't let us do what?"

"Waste the alien leader."

Flash cringed, disappointed in himself for being fooled by this woman. It was clear that she wasn't who she had pretended to be, and there was only one type of person who could hide who they are, and do it well enough to fool even him. "You're a Democrat."

She nodded.

"You pulled the mic out of the wall."

She nodded again.

"But you were at the anti-immigration protest."

She snorted. "Sure. As an Hispanic undocumented immigrant, I was there to protest the protesters."

"But your accent was fake." Flash said. "You're not even an undocumented immigrant, are you?"

"It's complicated but, technically, no. Look, I was born Sara White in a small town in Kansas. I mean, hello, can you get any more waspy and boring? It just didn't feel like that was the life I was meant to live. But then I see all these illegals--I mean undocumenteds--and the struggles they had. It was pretty cool. And I totally identified with them, because I struggled too. I mean, my struggles were a little different--they were white girl struggles, but still. Anyway, at that moment I became Maria Consuela Conchita Gonzales. I think it has a lot more pizazz."

"You identified with undocumented immigrants ... so you pretended to be one?"

Sara nodded.

"Let me get this straight," Guy said. "You've been pretending to be Maria Consuela Conchita Gonzales, but now you're Sara White again?"

Sara sighed in annoyance. "No. Yeah. Maybe. I don't know. I just know that I'm tired of the Hispanic thing." She paused a moment, deep in thought. "These zombies, I was scared of them this morning, before I knew they wouldn't eat me, but now--"

"Now you identify as a zombie?" Flash said.

"I think so," she said with a shrug. "Whatever." She rammed the butt of the shotgun into the basement room's only window, shattering it, and then used the barrel to ream away the broken pieces and clear the frame. A gust of fresh air rushed through the opening.

"There's a nice breeze. Probably won't take long for them to get here. They'll be able to smell your brains."

"The hell they will!" Guy lunged forward, but was jerked to a cold stop, restrained by the handcuffs like a dog on a short leash. Still, he didn't quit, continuing to try to stretch and grasp at Sara just inches from his reach.

But as Guy struggled, Flash thought. This woman was a wishy-washy Democrat if he ever saw one--and he had seen plenty. Maybe that was the ticket out of this mess. He knew she was no match for an intellect like his, and that he could probably talk his way out of this with half his brain tied behind his back.

"Look, Sara," he said, emphasizing her real name and not giving any credibility to her delusional Hispanic alias. "What have the Democrats ever done for you?"

"Really? You think you're going to talk your way out of this?"

Okay, this wasn't going to be easy. Wishy-washy or not, as a Democrat she was immune to logic and reason. He needed an emotional angle. Democrats can never resist their emotions.

"You're right. I can't talk my way out of this. I shouldn't even have tried. You're obviously a very smart, attractive woman." He smiled, pausing to let the words sink in. "You're also--"

"LGBTQ."

"Damn." Flash cringed. "Are you sure?"

Sara scoffed. "Umm, yeah, I think so," she said with a heavy dose of sarcasm. "I mean ... I *think* so," she said with a little less confidence.

"Because when we first met, fighting the zombies, I'm not so sure we didn't have a little chemistry." He looked her dead in the eyes. "Of course, someone as pretty--"

"Ok, enough," she said. But her words were softer--and a red glow flushed her cheeks.

"Fine," Flash said, not moving his gaze from her eyes. "I won't keep complimenting you. I'm sure you hear this kind of stuff all the time, anyway. What with your nice bright blue eyes, long brown hair--or is it chestnut?"

She twirled it. "I always thought it was more like auburn." She tried to suppress a giddy smile, but couldn't, and Flash knew he was on the right track.

They shared a stare that lingered into an awkward silence.

Flash leaned in.

Sara leaned in.

Their lips met. They kissed for a moment and then she stepped back, a smile and genuine look of wonder on her face.

"Woah," Guy said, his eyes wide. "Did that just change--are you no longer LPC--"

"LGBTQ," she snapped. "And don't be crazy. Probably more than ever, now!"

"Hey!" Flash said.

"Sorry. What I mean is, I do feel a little different. Something," she said. "Something is different. She paused, letting that something sink in. "I can't place my finger on it. Is it... happiness?"

"LPG...?" Guy tried again.

Flash gave Guy a look that told him to keep quiet. He wasn't completely sure what was going on here but it was some sort of transformation and he wanted to let it play out.

"Not so angry," Sara continued, "or irritated, or pessimistic. Maybe even a little *optimistic*."

"Free?" Flash asked, "To be an individual? Like you have value and control your own fate?"

"Yeah," she said with wonderment in her voice.

"I think that's conservatism," Flash said. He gestured to his handcuffs.

Sara unlocked the two men and, still in a bit of a haze, stepped back and leaned against the wall. Her hair blew gently in the soft breeze that came through the broken window above her. "It feels good. In fact, it feels--"

Two hands thrust through the open window, grabbed her by the sides of her head, and pulled her toward the outside until her shoulders stopped her by jamming against the window's frame. The sucking sound lasted only a moment. When it ended, Sara was dropped, lifeless, to the floor.

Flash and Guy looked at each other in horror. They knew they didn't have much time before she was back up and coming for them.

Flash grabbed the duffel bag, Guy grabbed the bazooka, and they were off.

***

Guy drove slowly along a path in the woods but stopped and parked his pickup truck a quarter-mile from the spaceship. The two men walked the rest of the way and settled behind the same bush, overlooking the spaceship, where they had hidden earlier.

In front of the ship, the zombie leader still sat at his table, picking at small stray pieces of leftover brain from the last meal.

Guy quietly opened the Bazooka case and then pulled the weapon up to his shoulder and flipped off the safety. "What do you say happens when he's blown to smithereens?" he asked as he poked the barrel through the bushes and adjusted the sights.

"Not sure, exactly," Flash said. "Maybe the rest of them drop dead on the spot. Maybe they return home. Maybe they just wander around like ... zombies, without someone doing their thinking for them."

"Drop dead on the spot sounds nice."

"Yeah, well, let's find out right now," Flash said, pointing beyond the ship to a long line of returning zombies. "Looks like it's feeding time again."

Guy took a deep breath and exhaled slowly. He pulled the trigger. There was a deafening explosion and a blistering burst of heat.

The blast burned a hole in the bush they were hiding behind. Through it, the men watched as the missile collided, not with the zombie leader, blowing him to bits, but with a force field that appeared, as if by magic, absorbing the shell and disintigrating it.

The zombie leader looked up to the source of the blast. The smoldering bush provided Flash and Guy no cover. Instantly, the line of zombies changed course and headed toward them.

Flash grabbed the duffel bag, ready to run. But Guy stood his ground and rolled up his sleeves.

"Don't be stupid," Flash said.

"Not stupid," Guy said. "Just patriotic."

"Come on. Live to fight another day."

Guy squinted and gave Flash a look of disbelief. "Doesn't that saying start with 'run away?'" He scoffed and stepped forward to meet the oncoming zombies.

"You go save your precious brain. I'm not running anywhere."

Guy towered over the creatures, just as he did most humans. His powerful punches landed, knocking the zombies back one by one. But each time, they came back. When one zombie on the ground grabbed Guy's legs, the big man lost his balance and fell.

Flash stepped back as a pile-on ensued. He shivered when the sucking sound permeated the air, then turned and sprinted back to the truck.

He tossed the duffel bag through the open window and onto the passenger seat before jumping in and turning the ignition.

The engine grinded and screeched, but wouldn't turn over.

He pounded the dashboard and tried again. "Come on, start," he screamed, pumping the gas pedal fast and furious.

Ahead, a gang of zombies were coming down the path on the way to the truck.

Flash checked the rear-view mirror. Zombies were coming from behind. He grabbed the duffel bag and threw open the door but, before getting out, realized he needed one more thing.

He leaned his body back as far as he could, braced against the front seat, and lifted his legs. He kicked the dashboard repeatedly, until it cracked just above the radio. He kicked it again and again, until it was shattered and he could wedge his fingers in to grab the radio. He ripped it out and stuffed it into the duffel bag.

The zombies were only about twenty yards away now, coming from the front and the rear.

Flash popped the hood. Sparks flew as he pulled the wires from the battery, and then he tossed it into the duffel bag, also.

The bag weighed a ton, and almost knocked him down as he threw it over his shoulder.

He raced deeper into the woods.

CHAPTER 4

Inside the Capitol, President Toobit stood behind the podium and addressed the closed-door session of the Senate. "It is true that we have been visited by beings from another planet."

A murmur arose from the crowd.

"But," the president said over the noise, "it is still unclear as to why they came or what they want."

"I respectfully disagree," called out Republican Senator Wilson Josephs in a forceful tone. The forty-eight Democrat senators on the floor turned in unison and scowled at him for breaking decorum, shaming him into an apology.

The president continued, "People are saying they are zombies. This is utter nonsense. They are simply beings who are looking for a better life. Our first step must be trying to understand them." He nodded to the back of the room where a row of military men, dressed in fatigues, locked and blocked the exits.

The captive crowd saw this and shifted nervously in their seats as a zombie was escorted to the front of the room next to the president. Toobit put his arm around the zombie's shoulder and smiled big as he leaned into the microphone. "Clearly, there is nothing to fear."

The audience remained silent and still.

"Senator Josephs," Toobit said, gesturing for him to come forward. "Please, see for yourself."

Josephs sat stiff until fellow senators began to nudge and encourage him. After a few moments of protesting, he reluctantly approached the zombie. Awkwardly unsure of how to greet the being, he extended his hand. The zombie grabbed it, then yanked the man forward and quickly grasped the sides of his head. He sniffed hard into the human's ear and then sucked out his brain.

The crowd screamed and jumped up in a panic. But the sight of the armed men, stationed in the rear, quieted the room and froze the senators.

Josephs, now a zombie, rose and started toward the crowd.

Toobit walked down the aisle to the door at the back of the room. The soldier guarding the door opened it, and then closed and locked it again after the president had exited.

Toobit waited just outside the locked Capital doors, enjoying the sounds from the annihilation of Republican lawmakers that was taking place inside. Like popcorn over a campfire, the screaming and banging reached a fever pitch before simmering to a stop.

He allowed himself a moment to fully appreciate what he had just orchestrated, and then continued to another podium that had been set up on the Capitol lawn. A row of military guards came and stood shoulder to shoulder behind the president. A sea of people waited in the street, on the other side of the metal security gate.

A man rushed the fence, screaming, "Alien, alien. You're an alien."

A group of people holding signs that read "Earthers Suck" and "Earth Sucks Too" pulled the man from the fence and threw him to the ground. They stomped and kicked him. The president waited patiently for the man to get back up, or for the stomping to end—whichever came first.

The stomping ended.

"As we are all aware," Toobit said to the crowd, "we have been visited by friends from another planet."

"They're zombies!" someone yelled. "Kill the zombies or they'll kill us!" This protestor was also met with swift action from a group carrying their own signs: "Zombie Lives Matter" and "Grey Matter Doesn't Matter."

The situation was resolved the same as the previous one and, when the stomping finally ended, the president continued.

"Now, they would not have come here if this were not an inherently better place than they left. That is simply common sense. So, we must not allow them to be treated like second-class citizens, like some kind of monsters from the sky. Remember, someday, we humans may advance to the point of space travel. And we may come in contact with others. When that day comes, we must be able to look back and know that we treated others the same way we want to be treated. That's not a human thing, or an alien thing, it is the right thing.

"Earlier today I introduced our friends from space to the House of Representatives and then to the esteemed members of our Supreme Court. Just minutes ago, they met the U.S. Senate. In the coming days, our government will be working hard to make sure that these people, and I will call them "people" from now on because there is no reason for to us put ourselves separate from them, or above them. So, these people will be treated with the dignity and respect that they deserve.

"Thank you and good afternoon."

***

When Flash finally stopped running he was deep in the woods. He dropped the duffel bag and peered back through the thick trees and bushes. It was quiet and still. No zombies were on his tail--at least for now. As he leaned up against a tree to catch his breath, he thought about Guy. What was the big man thinking? He had tried to pound it into Guy's head from the moment they met-- we can't fight them alone--but he just wouldn't listen.

Then again, what difference, at this point, did it make? The instant that thought popped into his head he cringed, the same way he did each time he heard the sound of a zombie sucking out a conservative brain. It did make a difference. It had too. Guy was fearless in his desire to fight for conservatism, and Flash was going to make sure that he didn't die in vain.

But the zombie population had grown exponentially and Flash knew that there was no way the Republicans could ever defeat them. Conservatives would always be outnumbered in this fight and, even if he could organize a rag-tag army, they would stand no chance. And, clearly, weapons were useless as even the bazooka's blast was absorbed by the alien's force field.

Dejected, he came to the realization that the only way these things would stop eating was when they ran out of food--when every conservative brain was gone. Then, of course, they would find some other planet to suck the life out of until it, too, was left a wasteland of brainless Democrats.

Then, it hit him. The epiphany. He laughed out loud at how stupid he had been to miss the solution that had been right under his nose the whole time--the only solution that would save conservatism.

Self-deportation.

If Republicans could deny the zombies of brains, not by actively fighting--which was a battle they were sure to lose--but by hiding out, the zombies would be forced to find another planet to feed on.

With renewed vigor, he pulled the truck radio and battery from the duffle bag, then dug through it for other supplies--a roll of copper wire, D cell batteries, and a walkie-talkie.

He smoothed out the bag and laid all his parts on it. It wasn't easy to work without the necessary tools, such as a solder gun and wire cutters, but with some ingenuity and the knowledge from a lifetime spent working with electronics, he was able to fashion what, hopefully, would be a working transmitter.

After lassoing a hundred feet of copper wire up to the top of the tallest tree he could find, he connected it all to the truck battery.

Static crackled immediately--a good sign--and he tuned the station. It was a crude setup that should work as a one-way transmitter--which meant he would have no way of knowing if anyone could hear him. But he took it on faith that someone out there was listening.

"With brilliance borrowed from God," he started. Then, he explained the strategy--keep yourself hidden, live in the shadows, and deny the zombies what they want.

***

President Toobit lined up an eight foot putt on the oval office floor, then stepped up to the ball and hovered over it, letting his club swing like a pendulum, feeling for just the right amount of power. He hadn't been putting worth a damn lately and was focused like a laser on getting his short game back on track.

He slowly drew the putter back when a knock on the door froze him.

"Christ!" He slammed the club into the ground repeatedly. The shaft split, leaving the head dangling at the end of it. "Who is it?"

"Dr. Philip Winslow," said a British man from behind the door.

Toobit rolled his eyes at the silly sounding accent. "Come in." He putted with his limp club, overshot wide and to the left of the plastic cup set up as the hole, and then tossed the club with disgust into the corner where it clanged against a coatrack and metal trash can before dropping to the floor. "What'd you find out?"

The doctor set his leather briefcase on top of a table in the corner. He unbuttoned his long plaid double-breasted tweed coat and removed his deerstalker hat--swapping it into his pocket for a monocle that he put into position on his left eye.

"As you know," the doctor said, "I am the world's finest neurosurgeon. But, more importantly, in this case, I am also the foremost authority on brain chemistry."

Toobit nodded, waiting for the interesting stuff.

"So, please understand that the tests I have conducted have been done with not only the latest scientific knowledge and state-of-the-art equipment, but with a greater basis of knowledge than exists anywhere in the world."

"I get it," Toobit said, rolling his hands to indicate 'get to the point.' "What did you learn?"

"Well. I have a couple of these beings at my lab and I have been able to ascertain quite a bit of information about them. It turns out that they're remarkably similar to us in many ways."

The president reached for the intercom on his desk. "Bring me a new putter. The XL2500. That's the one with the real leather grip, right?" He directed his attention back at the doctor. "Ok, I asked you to find out one simple thing."

"Right," the doctor said. "Can they vote? Well, they seem to possess no ability to think for themselves. Physically, they don't even have a brain, as they have been eaten. A few of them may have some remnants of brain if it wasn't sucked out completely--but there is no evidence that it would allow any sort of thinking as we define it. It seems all actions, aside from a limited number of instinctive abilities, come from some central source. A leader, I am led to believe, controlling them telepathically."

Toobit was awed. Telepathically controlling his followers would be a dream. No more speeches with hidden meanings. No more wink-wink nod-nod with the media. He allowed himself a few seconds to daydream of the possibilities and then got back to the doctor. "What if their leader told them how to vote?"

"I have no doubt that they would obey."

"Good," Toobit said. "Just what I needed to know." The president checked his watch. His 10am tee time was creeping up. "I think we're done."

"There is one more thing, Mr. President."

The British accent was beginning to grate on Toobit. He wasn't sure why. It just sounded silly. "What?" he snapped. "What is it?"

"Now, I understand that I was not commissioned for any other work but, well, I have information that I think you might find interesting."

Toobit checked his watch again. "Be quick."

"I have confirmed that these beings are, in fact, eating only conservative brains."

"I already knew that," Toobit said, impatiently motioning with his hands to move the conversation forward.

"I have identified the reason they like one type of brain over another. A very rare chemical compound--ruthenium sulfur hydrodioxide."

"Ruthen hydro doxa... huh?"

"Ruthenium sulfur hydrodioxide. The chemical shorthand is $RuSH_2O$. It's a trace chemical in the human brain, very difficult to detect and test for. As I said earlier, there is no one else in the world that could--"

"I get it. Go on."

"$RuSH_2O$ is the chemical responsible for activating portions of the brain that create conservative thought. It regulates, in a sense, a few core traits of conservative thought: honesty, integrity, intelligence--"

"Ok. Go on."

"Simply put, the more $RuSH_2O$ a person has, the more conservative they are."

"Really? Wow," Toobit said as he picked up the briefcase and handed it to the doctor, hurrying him out the door.

Winslow put the briefcase back on the table and opened it. "I've been able to synthesize $RuSH_2O$ in my lab." He grabbed a small vial, filled with a semi-transparent blue liquid, and held it up for the president to see. "I believe we can use this to satisfy the zombies' thirst for brains."

The president gave the doctor a puzzled look.

"We can save millions of lives," Winslow said.

"Republican lives?"

"Well, I suppose so. I mean, I didn't really consider who-"

"How much of this stuff do you have?"

Winslow gave a prideful smile. "I have a little more at my lab, but it is very easy to synthesize. And just a small drop equals what you would get from a human brain."

The president took the vial from Winslow and held it up to the light. If this liquid, with this $RuSH_2O$ stuff, was introduced to the zombie population, it would ruin his plans to destroy the Republican Party.

"Thank you for this, Mr. Winslow."

"*Doctor* Winslow," the doctor corrected.

Toobit scoffed. "So sorry, old chap," he said in a mocking British accent." He pressed the intercom on his desk and spoke into it. "Detain Sherlock Holmes."

Three Secret Service agents rushed into the room, threw the doctor to the ground, and handcuffed him. As they dragged him out, Toobit's caddy stepped around them and delivered the XL2500 leather-gripped putter to the president.

CHAPTER 5

Over the next couple of days, Flash's pirate broadcasts had reached much of his audience--at least those that had not already been transformed into brainless Democrats-- and as the truth about the alien zombies spread among Republicans, they took his advice to hunker down.

They remained barricaded behind locked doors and in makeshift basement bunkers. The freedom of the outdoors was now the domain of the Democrats and zombies. While Democrats continued life as usual, the zombies wandered the streets in search of food which, due to the Republicans successfully taking cover, was increasingly harder to come by.

***

Hozay walked along the quiet suburban road. His stomach grumbled. But worse than the pang from its emptiness was the disappointment and despair that washed over him. Once again, just as with every other planet he visited, this would not be the place he could call home. He looked up to God and asked why. He listened intently, hoping for a response, but heard nothing. The house-lined street he stalked remained dead silent--until a high-pitched static caught his ear.

He knew sounds like this didn't happen by themselves. It meant that a human--food--must be near, so he followed the noise. The crackly electric whining led him up a house's walkway to the front door, where it continued to buzz on the other side. He pounded, kicked, and pushed on the wooden door until its hinges gave in. Then, he threw the door open and stepped inside.

The wondrous smell of one of this planet's delectable brains instantly engulfed him. He inhaled, long and slow, enjoying the dwelling's welcoming aroma like freshly baked cookies just out of the oven.

The terrified man in the house stepped in front of a woman, blocking her from danger. He threw a small radio--the source of the static--at the alien's head.

It smashed against Hozay's face, but the alien ignored it. Good meals had become hard to come by and the delicious scent was all he could concentrate on.

As the static continued to screech from the radio on the floor, he reached down and grabbed the man by the sides of the head. He pulled his next meal up, placed his mouth over the man's ear, and began to suck.

In the background, the static stopped, and then words came across the radio.

"With brilliance borrowed from God."

Hozay froze as the word "God" hung in the air. He dropped the human and picked up the small radio. He raised it to his ear, afraid to miss a word. Of course, he didn't understand the rest of the words that followed, but he understood the word "God," and this could only mean one thing. God was speaking to him.

Pits of anxiety replaced the hunger pangs in his stomach. Had he done something wrong? Was God angry with him? He looked at the human whose brain he was about to eat and knew--because he had a mind of his own and the ability to think--that God didn't want him to do it. God was telling him that this *was* the place that would be his home.

But Hozay knew that if this was going to be his home, he would have to learn to be like the humans. And he *wanted* to be like the humans. He wanted to dress like them. He wanted to talk like them. And he especially wanted to eat like them.

He marched into the kitchen and frantically pulled the doors off every cabinet and fished around inside for food, clumsily sending plates and glasses to shatter on the floor. When he finally found a cabinet with boxes of food, he smelled them. Each box had its own aroma. Some were sweet, others were stale, and others he couldn't figure out. It wasn't the fresh food he was used to, but this is what God wanted him to eat, because this is what the humans eat.

He opened the first box and poured the contents into his mouth before tossing it to the side. The crunchy food tickled his mouth. It was fun. He grabbed the next box, ripped the top off and poured the powdery food into his mouth. This was dry, and made him thirsty. He went through all of the boxes, and then the cans, cracking them open with his hands and sucking out the inside.

When the cabinet was bare, he opened the refrigerator and grabbed cartons one by one, chugging them until empty and tossing the empty container to the floor. Then, he moved on to the other bowls and plates full of food.

A thought command interrupted him: bring food.

Hozay ignored the command. He continued eating, devouring everything in sight. Soon, the refrigerator was empty--but the alien's stomach was full.

***

President Toobit trudged along the untrodden path through the woods, using his five iron to slap branches away from his face as he went. "How much further is it?" he whined to Jacket, the leader of the two-person expedition who was twenty paces ahead. "I don't have all day for this." He swiped away a flurry of gnats and continued on until, ahead in a clearing, he could see the alien spaceship. In front of it, seated at a table, was an alien. Toobit stopped in his tracks. "Is that who I think it is?"

"Yes," Jacket said. "He's the leader."

Butterflies fluttered in the president's stomach as he stared at the being in awe. This was the one who was going to wipe out Republicans for all eternity. A tear flowed down each cheek and a lump formed in his throat. He swallowed hard. "He's beautiful," he said with a sniffle.

"We've been trying to communicate with him, to get him to tell his followers to vote for you. But all he does is make a bunch of strange sounds."

In the distance, a long single-file line of zombies emerged from the woods. "What's going on there?" the president asked.

"Must be feeding time," Jacket said. "Get a load of this."

The first zombie approached the table and tried to vomit, but could only dry heave. After gagging and coughing, he stuck his finger down his throat to help, but it just brought on more fruitless heaving.

The leader turned his sights to the next zombie in line who approached the table but also failed to vomit any food.

After more failed attempts by the next zombies in line, the leader stood and flipped the table over in anger. With an enraged look on his face, he stared hard at his followers standing before him, switching his furious gaze from one to another.

A moment later, the spaceship's door opened and the leader pointed to it. The zombies began to file into the ship.

"What's going on?" Toobit asked.

"I don't know," Jacket said. "It looks like they're leaving."

Panic washed over the president. "No. Don't leave," he cried as he sprinted down the small hill toward the ship. "Please. Don't leave!" He stumbled and fell, tumbling the rest of the way down the incline, banging against rocks and getting poked by twigs as he rolled. When he stopped, he found himself at the feet of the alien.

He quickly stood, face-to-face with the leader, and brushed himself off.

He bowed.

A long, deep bow.

He held in the bowed position, unsure what kind of bow this leader from another planet would require.

"I think that's long enough," Jacket said after she had made her way down the hill.

Toobit finished his bow and stood erect. "Do you know who I am?" he asked.

The zombie responded: Click. Click-clack. Clack clack clacky-click.

"See?" Jacket whispered. "He just makes those weird clicking sounds."

"Weird?" Toobit said. "No. Those are the most beautiful sounds in the world." But he had not heard them since he was a child. It made him think of that cherished time when, as a young boy, he would spend his days as a footballer in the hot sun, and his nights relaxing with nyanya's sweet goat-milk pudding.

Click-click clicky clacky-clack click went the president to say: How do you know this language?

A slew of clicks and clacks in response translated to: I always speak the native language of a planet's leader.

Back and forth they went, clicking and clacking.

"Why are you leaving?" Toobit asked.

"We came here for food. We did not come to struggle for it, or to suffer, or to be denied what we want."

"Denied? I would never deny you anything?"

"We want the brains from the humans. But the humans run. They hide."

Toobit clenched his fists in anger. "Heartless Republican bastards," he said to himself. He turned to Jacket. "What is this all about?"

"Must be Lambo, sir. He's hiding out in these woods somewhere and still broadcasting. He's sending the message to his listeners to take cover, to hide. Every time we block his frequency he moves to another one."

Toobit turned back to the zombie leader and clicked: I understand your frustration. But please know that they are not my people. My people want you to have what you came for. In fact, I'm going to see to it that you get what you came for.

"This is a matter of civil rights, isn't it?" he asked Jacket. "I mean, you can't just stop someone from eating because you don't like what they eat. I don't like hotdogs or apple pie, but I don't stop anyone from eating them, do I?"

"No. Although we do tax the hell out of those things."

"But they can still eat them."

"That is true."

"I want to round up every one of these civil rights violators. Free up space in the jails for them."

"How much space should we free up?"

Toobit thought for a moment. "All of it. Whoever's in there now has probably been there long enough."

"And find Lambo," he added. "Don't just block his broadcasts, I want him in jail with the others."

He addressed the alien leader with a series of clicks to say: Don't worry. You're going to get what you came for.

The alien clicked back to say thanks.

The president bowed.

CHAPTER 6

The staticky feedback quieted. Flash tapped the walkie-talkie speaker he was using as a mic. The batteries were finally dead and, with no replacement, that meant his broadcasts had come to an end.

He tossed the contraption that was his transmitter to the side and leaned back against a tree, wondering if his broadcasts had even been received. There was only one way to find out--get back to the city and see for himself what was going on.

After a long walk through the woods, he crossed a highway and arrived at the outskirts of a small suburban town. Zombies roamed the quiet streets. There weren't many, just a handful in this sparsely populated area. But he took the lull in the town as a good sign--that Republicans had heard, and heeded, his advice to hunker down. He was easily able to avoid the few scattered zombies as he continued through the suburb and approached the city limit. As he got closer, he heard a low rumbling which, by the time he was just a short distance away, was clearly recognizable as the sounds of a celebration in the streets.

He worked his way behind the American Airwaves building and peeked around the corner. A giant banner spanned the street. It read: "Zombie Pride." A procession of convertibles, with zombies piled inside, drove slowly down the street. On the sides, thousands of Democrat citizens cheered and danced as music blasted in the background.

On every corner, for as far as he could see, vendors distributed zombie-related paraphernalia such as t-shirts, hats, and mugs, with slogans like "Zombies are People Too" and "Zombie is the new Human." Judging by the attire of the crowd, the items were a hit. The hottest selling item, however, appeared to be from the food vendors--a thick and chunky syrupy mix that could be sucked out of a plastic skull and provided a realistic brain-sucking experience for the true zombie enthusiast. Not a single Democrat toddler could pass by the display without pestering his or her parents for "just one more 'publican brain"--and not a single one was denied.

Flash studied the zombie Mardi Gras a little longer, amazed at how quickly and thoroughly the brain-eating creatures had been mainstreamed.

Then, suddenly, his hands were yanked behind his back. Cold metal handcuffs pinched his wrists as they clicked shut. "You're under arrest, Lambo," said a voice from behind.

"Arrest? What for?" He struggled, unsuccessfully, to turn around.

"Pirate radio," said a second man, dressed in army fatigues, who stepped in front.

"Pirate radio? That's only a fine."

"As of last night it's a felony," his captor said. "The zombie congress voted on it."

***

The line of Republicans, dressed in orange jumpsuits and chained together at the ankles, stretched across the prison courtyard. A single guard, with his billy club in hand, sauntered along the line, eyeing each prisoner from head to toe as he went, trying to decide if the conservative in front of him should be chosen as the last participant for the game.

The rules of the game were simple. Five zombies and five Republicans roaming free in the yard. The zombies' goal was to get the brains. The conservatives' goal was to survive--and the last one to have his brain eaten was the winner.

The guard stopped between two prisoners. "Which one will it be?" He tapped each Republican on the shoulder with his club as he recited "eeny, meeny, miney, moe." When he finished, the chosen one was unshackled and shoved into the center of the yard with the four other Republican participants. Another guard pinned the number five on the contestant's back.

As the rest of the conservatives were ushered back inside to their cells, a bustling mob of spectators filed into the yard and congregated on the side. One man went to the front of the crowd. "Place your bets," he called.

He was instantly swarmed and surrounded by the boisterous horde.

"Ten bucks on number two to go down first!"

"I got twenty on number four!"

"Number three looks scrappy. Fifty on him!"

Money flew, and the bookie worked furiously to collect it all until the action was settled. Then, a piercing siren sounded and five zombies were released into the yard.

The mob cheered.

The Republicans spread out to avoid the zombies. Five against five didn't seem like bad odds, especially considering that the zombies had no brains and couldn't strategize. But, although they weren't smart enough to work together, they didn't tire, and they chased their prey around the yard relentlessly.

When contestant number three was corned by two zombies, due to sheer bad luck, he was the first to lose. The zombies sucked, together, one in each ear, and then dropped the Republican to the ground.

The crowd erupted.

There was another rush to the bookie as bettors looked to take advantage of the changed odds--it was now six versus four.

The game wore on and, as designed, the situation worsened for the remaining Republicans: seven against three, eight against two, and then, finally, nine against one.

When the final conservative fell, the last of the bets were paid. The spectators, drained from the excitement, left the yard. One man was particularly glum. "I lost every time. How is that even possible?"

"Forget about it," a friend consoled. "You'll do better tomorrow."

Flash lay on his back, staring at the concrete ceiling of his 7x9 cell. His legs dangled over the end of the small cot, the springs of which he could feel through the thin disintegrating mattress.

"Lights out," a voice echoed. The cell block went black for a moment before a few small fluorescent lights in the main hallway flickered to life, giving the area a dark and creepy ambience. The hum of the bulbs was the only sound to be heard in the eerie silence.

Flash remained on his back and drifted deep into thought. How ironic that he, the ultimate defender and professor of freedom, would spend his final days in prison before having his brain and mind destroyed--devoured--by a Democrat zombie.

Approaching footsteps caught his attention and he listened intently as they stopped at the neighboring cell. "Come on, McCall," a guard said. The cell door screeched open. "It's feeding time."

"Feeding time?"

"Yeah, as in you're the meal. You know the drill."

There was a scuffle, some banging, and then a zap-- what sounded like a taser--followed by the heavy thud of a body hitting the ground. A moment later, the guard crossed in front of Flash's cell, dragging an unconscious McCall by the foot. When they were further down the corridor, the prisoner must have regained his senses as he could be heard struggling to get free, but another zap quickly put an end to it. Silence returned, and the hum of the lights was once again all that could be heard.

As Flash lay there thinking about his fate, and the fate of his fellow jailed conservatives, his attention was soon grabbed again. This time, by a sound that was fainter and further away--whispering voices that came, not from out in the hallway or a neighboring cell, but from the vent in the corner of his cell.

He kneeled by the vent and listened to the whispered conversation.

"Any pattern to who they're taking to feed the zombies?" one dispirited voice said in a hushed tone. "I'm in Block C. They took the guy across from me this morning."

"No. It seems random," another whispered back. "I'm in Block A and they took eight of us last night."

"Block D, here," someone else chimed in. "Three gone so far tonight."

"What do you think it's like? Having your brain sucked out."

"I don't know. But they say that when it happens, you become a Democrat."

"Are you serious? I figured you just die."

"I wish. But you never die."

"You mean, you're a Democrat for the rest of your life."

"Worse. For all of eternity."

It was clear that the conservatives' spirits were weakened and, while there was nothing Flash could do to change the situation, he did what came naturally. He put his mouth up to the metal grate and spoke is a strong whisper. "With brilliance borrowed from God."

A few chuckles emanated from the vent. "Is that really you, Flash?" someone asked.

"The one and only. Now listen. Things may seem hopeless, but this isn't over until we lose our spirit, and I'm not going to let that happen. The spirit of conservatism which, we all know, is what fuels the spirit of freedom, can't be destroyed by Democrats, zombies, aliens, whatever you want to call them. So, it's going to be my job to keep that spirit alive. In order to do that ... I welcome you to the most intelligent and educational entertainment anywhere across the fruited plains."

Hunched over in the corner of his cell and whispering into the air vent, Flash continued talking. Jailed conservatives chimed in from all across the prison and soon, it seemed, the entire population was listening. If the end was near, Flash couldn't think of a better way to spend his final days, hours, or minutes, than by doing what he loved most.

But it all ended when his cell door screeched open.

He turned to a blinding flashlight shining in his eyes.

"Show's over, Lambo," a voice growled from behind the beam of light. "Get up."

CHAPTER 7

The black-tie gala, celebrating the Republican extinction, packed the White House Ballroom with the country's most prominent Democrats. The evening kicked off with a lavish cocktail hour where guests mingled, joked, and enjoyed the festive mood. But the buzz in the air was all about the evening's live entertainment--the embossed invitations had promised "a fantastic display of transformation, from Republican to Democrat before your very eyes."

With dinner about to be served, President Toobit, standing behind the dais, lifted his glass and tapped it repeatedly with his fork. The clinking quickly silenced the room and all eyes turned to him.

"Thank you all for joining me tonight on this most joyous and momentous occasion. When I became president, I said the following in my acceptance speech ..." He gestured to a worker who rolled a teleprompter into the middle of the room, and then the president continued, reading an excerpt from his acceptance speech as it scrolled on the teleprompter.

"I promise to change the tone in Washington. To end the partisan bickering. To unite us, not as Democrats and Republicans, but as one party." He gestured to the worker again, and the teleprompter was rolled out.

"Well, it looks like that will actually happen. The tone will change. The bickering will end. We will all be united as a single party." Then, after a dramatic pause and with added emphasis, continued, "the *Democratic* Party."

Cheers and applause rose from the crowd, and the president waited for it to die down before he continued. "Before we eat, I would like to bring in the man ... the person ... the being, who has helped to make this happen. Please welcome our guest of honor, the one we have been waiting for."

At the side of the room, a set of double doors opened. A spotlight shined down and the zombie leader entered. The crowd, once again, erupted into wild applause.

The alien stumbled and staggered across the floor, and a hush smothered the cheering. Struggling to keep his balance, the zombie made his way to the dais and flopped into his seat.

"He doesn't look too good," someone in the crowd called out.

Toobit took a close look at the zombie alien. His eyes were glassy and bloodshot, his skin more pale and clammy than usual, and his breathing labored.

Mo Lester, sandwiched between two women, one under each arm, called, "I know that look." He chuckled. "It's called 'too much of a good thing.'"

While the crowd gawked at the sickly alien, Toobit turned to Jacket. "Maybe Lester's right. Can too much brain be bad for you?"

Jacket shrugged. "I don't know. We've been pulling a couple dozen Republicans out of jail each day for him. I guess it is a bit excessive."

"And the conditions in the jail--no clean water, no soap or working showers, barely any food." Toobit grimaced. "Maybe the meat is tainted."

A ruckus in the back of the room commanded everyone's attention as two white-gloved workers forced McCall into the room. He was dressed in his orange prison jumpsuit, gagged, and his wrists and ankles were chained together.

Toobit cringed when he saw the prisoner--the zombie alien's meal for the evening's exhibition. As excited as he was to show off the fantastic display of the transformation--from Republican to Democrat before their very eyes--he couldn't risk the alien's well-being.

He jumped in front of the alien to block the view of his potential victim. If he was sick, whether from over-indulgence or food poisoning or something unrelated, the prudent thing to do was to stop him from eating. "Get him out of here," the president called to the workers about McCall. "This isn't a good time."

But it was too late. The zombie lifted his nose into the air and sniffed deep. Even in his sickly state he could smell the brain from across the room. He grunted as he forced himself out of his chair.

Toobit tried to hold the alien back but the zombie tossed the president to the side. Like an angry drunken Kennedy, he pushed his way through the crowd until he reached the Republican. He grabbed the man's head and placed his mouth over one of his eyes. As he sucked, he covered the victim's mouth to mute the screaming. A loud pop echoed throughout an otherwise hushed room, and then the alien spit out an eyeball. After the crowd watched it bounce and roll across the floor, the alien sucked the conservative's brain through the eye socket and then dropped the lifeless body.

The partygoers gasped in awe, then cheered and applauded.

But a moment later, the alien zombie swayed. He took a step back and then fell to the ground with a thud, landing next to his victim.

In a panic, Toobit raced to the back of the room. He kicked McCall's lifeless body out of the way and kneeled next to the alien, shaking him by the shoulders as he cried, "No. No. Why did you do it?"

The zombie's eyes rolled over and he convulsed.

"Get Dr. Winslow," Toobit cried. "Now!"

***

The guard shoved Flash into the solitary confinement cell. "Enjoy your new studio," he said as he slammed the steel door shut.

It took a moment for Flash's eyes to adjust to the darkness of the dank, musty room. But when they did, he found himself in an even more confined, more dreary cell than his first one--a concrete box with a solid steel door, save for the small feeding hole at the bottom of it which let in the only trace of light.

"Nice to meet you, neighbor," came a voice with a British accent from the next cell.

Flash kneeled and put his face to the small opening at the bottom of the door. "Who are you?"

"Philip Winslow. Doctor Philip Winslow. Been here a week. I think. Sure is nice to hear a voice. So, what's your name."

"It's Flash."

"Is that a first name or a last name?"

"You don't know who I am?"

"No. Should I?"

"In a prison full of conservatives, I didn't think I could be anonymous."

"Well, I'm not a conservative."

"Then why are you in here?"

"I'm a doctor, like I said. A neurosurgeon with a specific bent toward brain chemistry. A few days ago, I went to the president with a way to stop the zombies from eating human brains, but it turns out the president didn't want to hear it." He sighed. "Guess he didn't want anyone to hear it."

"So what is it--this way to stop them from eating brains?"

"I've identified a rare chemical in the human brain called ruthenium sulfur hydrodioxide."

"Ruthenium sulfur hydrodioxide? What does it do?"

"Simply put, the more conservative you are, the more of this chemical is in your brain. The less conservative, the less of the chemical. It's this very chemical that provides

71

the nourishment for these creatures. It's what they crave. It's what they need. I was able to create a serum, a liquid, with an enormously concentrated amount of $RuSH_2O$. Feeding it to the zombies would have completely satisfied their desire for human brains."

"You should have known Toobit wouldn't want that serum. It would spare conservative lives."

"I didn't think that way. I am a man of science, and science isn't political."

"To Democrats it is."

"Yes, well, it appears to be so. But I still believe that someday my work can be used to help others. Many, many others as the case may be."

"Unfortunately, I don't think we will ever get to see that day."

"Mr. Flash, if anything happens to me, and by some chance you find yourself free of all of this, my formula is in my lab at 504 Bean Street."

"I'm sure that, by now, the Toobit administration has visited your lab and stolen all of your work."

"Yes, you are probably correct. But I do have one sample that they would not have found. I've hidden an unlabeled vial--sort of a secret backup, safe from prying eyes. You'll find it under a loose floorboard of the closet at the rear of the room. Find that vial and any competent scientist will be able to reverse engineer the product."

As echoing footsteps from out in the hall grew closer, Flash waited, listening. The door to Winslow's cell screeched open. "Let's go, doc," said a guard. "The president wants you."

***

Dr. Winslow kneeled beside the zombie, who lay on its side, in the fetal position, moaning, groaning, and barely moving. He opened his black medical bag and fished inside for his monocle--which he placed over his eye, and a large needle--which he inserted deep into the zombie's stomach. With a slow steady pull, a milky liquid was extracted from the alien's stomach and into the needle's vial. A single drop of the liquid placed onto a test strip quickly changed the strip's color from white to bright red.

"Just as I suspected," the doctor said. "He's overdosing on $RuSH_2O$." He stood and addressed the crowd that was circled around him. "$RuSH_2O$ is a chemical in the brain. The more conservative--"

"We get it," Toobit interrupted. He was clearly agitated and nervous. "Are you sure about this? I mean, that's all they do is eat brains. Isn't their body used to it? They must be used to it. He has to be ok. Right?"

"The brains that he has been consuming have a much higher concentration of $RuSH_2O$ than any they have encountered in the thousands of other galaxies they have visited. And, they have been eating far more of them. Both the quality and quantity of $RuSH_2O$ are killing him."

"Killing him?" Toobit cried.

73

Winslow held the test strip up. "This tells me he has almost ten times the amount of $RuSH_2O$ in his body as when I first tested these beings. Ten times! He's lucky to be alive ... dead ... undead ... whatever .... You get my point."

"So, what do we do now?" Toobit asked. "How do we fix this? We can fix it, right?"

"There is only one solution. He must not ingest any more $RuSH_2O$. None. At this point, even a single drop could be fatal."

The word 'fatal' stuck Toobit like a dagger. "For how long? When can he start eating brains again? He will be able to eat brains again, right?"

"It's hard to say, exactly. But at least a couple of days. At that point I'll need to test him again to see if his levels have dropped."

"Are you sure that his levels will drop?"

"So long as no more $RuSH_2O$ --and I mean not a single drop--gets into his system, his levels will drop and he will be fine. But, should any $RuSH_2O$ get into this being's system--"

"Stop!" the president interrupted as he covered his ears with his hands. "I don't need to hear any more."

"It's imperative that you understand the consequences," Winslow continued. "Any more $RuSH_2O$ --"

"La-la-la-la-la-la-la," the president repeated loudly, drowning out the doctor. "I don't hear you."

When Winslow's mouth stopped moving, Toobit lowered his hands. He took a deep breath to calm himself. "I think a couple of days is doable." After another calming breath, he nodded to the guard that had escorted the doctor in. "Take him back now."

CHAPTER 8

"How about that approach shot on the fourteenth?" Toobit said to his caddy as they walked down the White House hallway.

"One of your best of the day, sir."

"Yes," the president said. "One of them." He stopped outside the Lincoln Bedroom and checked his watch before opening the door. "Think we can squeeze in one more round?"

"I thought you were busy--staff meetings and zombie stuff."

"It's a perfect day out there. Seems a shame to waste it."

"You do have a point."

"The meeting can wait. Let me just check on you-know-who."

Inside the room, the zombie hadn't moved since Toobit left him that morning. He still lay in bed, on his side, facing the rear wall. He pulled the covers up to his neck and let out a long deep groan.

The president scanned the room for the two guards that were tasked with making sure the alien didn't sneak any brains, but they were not in the room.

A soft breeze rippled the curtains that covered a set of French doors which led to an outside terrace. A zombie clumsily tip-toed through the doors, toward the leader, and vomited food on the edge of the bed.

"No," Toobit yelled as he rushed to the side of the bed. He pushed the zombie back through the terrace doors and out of the room. Outside, a long line of zombies waited. The president slammed the doors shut, locked them, and drew the curtains.

He stomped over to the bed and pulled the covers down, revealing a messy mound of brain stashed under the blankets. "You know you can't have this," he reprimanded the alien with a flurry of clicks. He grabbed a towel from the nightstand and used it to push the pile of brain onto the floor. "Get a mop on this," he called to the guards.

Click-clack! Clacky-click click, the leader said to Toobit angrily.

"No," Toobit clicked back. "Not until the doctor checks you again."

Click clack-clicky, click clack cluck.

"Just a couple of more days," Toobit clicked back.

He set his attention back to the missing guards wondering where they were. Music and giggling from an adjoining suite clued him in to their whereabouts.

"What the hell is going on?" he said as he stomped over to the connected room and threw the door open. Inside, the two guards, Mo Lester, and three women were seated around a poker table.

"Full house," one of the women said, laying her cards face up on the table--three queens and a pair of eights.

"That beats my pair of tens," Lester said with a smile. He undid his tie, twirled it in the air like a lasso and tossed it off to the side. He took a sloppy sip from his cocktail glass which was filled to the brim. "Whose deal?"

"No one's," Toobit yelled as he wiped the table clear, sending cards fluttering and drinking glasses crashing to the floor. "And get these girls out of here."

"Sheesh. Get a load of President Buzzkill," Lester said to the women, who giggled and flung their arms around him.

"You too, Lester." He stuck his finger in the ex-President's face. "I don't need you anymore. I don't need your political advice. I don't even need you to make me look good to the voters." He pointed to the other room where the alien leader lay. "I've got my golden goose, and it's not you anymore." He put his fingers to his mouth and blew a loud whistle. Secret Service agents rushed through the door, manhandled Lester, and dragged him away.

"You can't do this," Lester yelled as the agents pulled him out the door and dragged him down the hallway. "I have to be here. I need to be here," he repeated over and over until he was out of earshot.

"Do your job," Toobit said to the guards. He shook his head in disappointment and then checked his watch and turned to his caddy. "Let's squeeze in a round."

***

The cell door's latch snapped open with a loud clink that hung in the air as light poured into the room for the first time in days. Flash's eyes struggled to adjust, although he didn't need to see anything--he knew exactly what this visit meant.

"It's feeding time," the guard said as he stepped into the cell. "Move it."

Flash got to his feet, ready to fight. He had no intention of going quietly. If he was going to die, or worse, be transformed into a brainless Democrat, he wasn't going to make it easy on them. He didn't have much of a plan, though--just fight. If he could manage his way out of the cell, he would take it from there.

As the guard took another step forward, Flash pushed off the back wall and lunged at him.

He was met with the thwack of the guard's billy club into his shoulder. The stinging pain knocked him back a step and, in that moment, the guard stepped forward and jammed a taser into Flash's neck.

As fifty thousand volts shot through him, every muscle in his body spasmed violently. He could feel the electricity coursing through every inch of his body, up to his head, down to his toes, even through his teeth.

The shock ended a few seconds later and he slumped to the floor--a pile of mush, unable to move, speak, or even think. His body was still tingling from the shock as he slipped out of awareness and everything went black.

When he came to, he found himself in an infirmary bed, his legs and arms secured at his side with leather straps, buckled tight. The room was cold, and it smelled of disinfectant. There was a row of beds to his left and right, and all were filled with prisoners who were also strapped down.

A doctor, wearing a white lab coat and holding a clipboard, approached his bed. "Lambo?" he read off the chart in his hand before placing it at the foot of the bed. "You're the guy on the radio, right?" He examined Flash's eyes and ears with a small flashlight.

Flash didn't respond, but the doctor didn't seem to care, or even expect an answer.

He cleaned Flash's shoulder with an alcohol swab and then unwrapped a needle from its plastic package. He held it up and tapped it with his index finger a few times, then squeezed until a small drop overflowed from the tip. "Just an antibiotic," he said, still with the same tone that made it clear he expected it to be a one-way conversation. "The president doesn't want to introduce any tainted food into the zombie population." He stuck the needle into Flash's shoulder and delivered the medicine, then dropped the needle into a trashcan. "I'll be back in about an hour," he said as he checked his watch. "We'll give you a light sedative. It makes the final process a little easier for everyone."

"The final process?" Flash said. "Is that what you call a zombie sucking someone's brain out of their head? A process?"

"Mr. Lambo," the doctor said, "try not to get yourself all worked up. It increases the lactic acid in the body and affects the way things taste." He checked his watch again.

"I'll see you in an hour." He hung the clipboard on the edge of the bed and then he walked away.

One hour. That's all he had left. Then, the *process* would begin. No doubt he would remain tied up and, apparently, sedated, throughout. But he didn't think about the process, or how much pain he would feel, or even what it would be like after getting transformed into a brainless Democrat. Because none of that mattered. At this point, there was only one thing that mattered-- conservatism would soon be extinguished. He tried to keep images of a conservative-less country, of a conservative-less world, from invading his thoughts, but he couldn't.

"Flash," someone said in a low whisper next to him. "I had a feeling I'd find you here. You have to help me."

Flash instantly recognized the gravelly southern-drawled voice and turned to see Mo Lester kneeling by his bed.

"You gotta help me," he repeated in a desperate tone.

Flash gave Lester an incredulous look and pulled at his leather restraints. "I have to help *you*?"

"Toobit banished me from the White House." His voice was shaking, and his words frantic. "I can't get in there again. Ever. I need to be in there. I need to party there." He clutched Flash's arm. "If anyone can stop him, I know you can. You can stop any Democrat."

"There's only one way to stop Toobit, and that's by stopping these zombies."

Lester scoffed. "There's tens of thousands of them by now. This is really something that should have been done sooner."

Flash rolled his eyes. "That's why I came to you when this all started."

"You're right. I admit it. I should have ..." his voice trailed off as something at the far end of the room caught his attention. "Who is that cute little redhead down there?" he said, craning his neck to peer toward the end of the room. "Already sedated and tied?"

"Lester!" Flash whispered.

"You're right. I'm sorry. Go on. I'm paying attention."

"We can't worry about all of the zombies. We just need to get rid of the leader."

"Good luck with that. Since he got sick, he's so heavily guarded no one can get to him."

"Sick? Sick how?"

"RuSH^{2}O poisoning. The doctor said one more drop'll kill him." He shook his head. "Too bad we don't have any of it."

Flash's eyes lit up. "I know where to get it."

"Where? I know a guy that can finish this job, and he's good. I guarantee it'll be an accident." The word 'accident' was in air quotes and followed by a wink.

"No. You need to get me out of here. If I send you to get it, the first good-looking woman that crosses your path will make you forget what you're supposed to be doing."

"Now that is not fair," Lester said indignantly. "I can take this seriously." He paused for a moment. "But what are we talking--blonde, brunette?" He stretched to look down the end of the room. "Fiery little redhead like my girl down there?"

"Lester! Get me out of here."

"Ok. But I can't just untie you and walk you out of here. Everyone knows who you are. You'll need a disguise."

"A disguise? Where am I going to get a disguise."

Lester smiled. "I might have something in my car. You know, something I keep on hand in case of an emergency. What do you want? Policewoman, nurse ... naughty schoolgirl?"

Flash rolled his eyes. "Nurse, I guess. That would probably make the most sense."

"Good choice," Lester said. "Be back in a jiff."

CHAPTER 9

Winslow's lab had been ransacked. Every door and cabinet remained open and the floor was littered with their contents. Tables had been overturned, volumes of binders and notebooks shredded, and racks of chemicals flipped. The spilled chemicals had combined on the floor and reacted, creating a rancid smoky haze that lingered in the air.

Flash and Lester scanned the room, assessing the rubble, and then spoke at the same time:

"Democrats," Flash said, shaking his head in disgust.

"Nicely done," Lester said with a nod of approval.

Flash navigated the debris strewn about the floor and found the closet at the rear of the room. Just as Winslow had assured, a single unmarked vial of RuSH^{2}O lay hidden under a loose floorboard.

Lester grabbed a lab coat and deerstalker hat from a hanger and tossed it to Flash. "This should get you into the White House."

Flash shed the nurse's outfit. He put on Dr. Winslow's coat and hat and then found a monocle in the coat's pocket and fitted it over his left eye. He rested the vial, conservatism's only hope, safely in his pocket.

***

Flash drove up to the security checkpoint where a guard came to his window.

"Dr. Philip Winslow," he said in his best British accent. "Here to treat the alien zombie leader."

The guard checked his clipboard, flipping through a few pages. "Sorry, but I have you scheduled for tomorrow afternoon." He pointed up ahead to a bend in the road. "You can turn around over there."

"I'm afraid there's been an emergency. The poor chap is really quite under the weather. And the president has made it very clear to me that I do not want to be the one to stand in the way of his getting better."

The guard thought about it for a moment.

"You know how he can get his knickers in a twist when he doesn't get his way," Flash continued. "Just between you and me, of course, I don't think either of us wants to be on the receiving end of that."

The guard pondered Flash's words another moment and then handed him a visitor's tag and waved him on.

After another layer of inept security at the entrance to the White House, Flash made his way to the main corridor and focused on the directions to the Lincoln Bedroom that Lester had given him: across the south wing to the bust of Woodrow Wilson, take a left, third door on the right. Not completely confident in his disguise, he kept his head down as he hurried. When he reached his destination, he stopped in front of the oak door and took a deep breath to compose himself. The stakes were high. No matter what happened, he had to get the RuSH^{2}O into the alien. Failure was not an option.

He knocked firmly. An armed guard answered and stood in the doorway.

"I'm here to evaluate the patient," Flash said in a confident and forceful tone.

The guard looked at Flash suspiciously and then leaned back and called into the room, "Mr. President, the doctor is here to see the alien."

Flash's stomach dropped. The plan to get inside the White House had been conceived in such a rush that, foolishly, he had not thought about the possibility of Toobit being in the room.

"Ok, let him in," the president said.

Flash kept his head down as he entered, peeking up just enough to get a read of the room. At the far left side was a bed. A large lump, no doubt the alien, lay beneath the covers. To the right, Toobit stood before a mini indoor putting green, engrossed in the practice of his short game. "Checking his RuSH^{2}O levels?" he asked as he sent the ball left of the hole.

"Uh, yes, Mr. President," Flash said in his English accent. "And a smidge of medicine."

Toobit looked up from the green and stared hard at Flash through squinted eyes. He took a step forward and lifted his putter, pointing it at the visitor.

Flash slowly reached his hand into his pocket, clutching the vial. He made a quick note of the positioning of the two guards and was confident he could rush the alien from this distance. If need be, he would quickly force-feed the chemical to the zombie.

"You," Toobit said with an angry voice, "have the dumbest sounding accent I have ever heard. I can't take it anymore. I mean, seriously, why can't you people talk normal like everyone else?"

A bunch of clicking sounds came from under the covers on the bed: Click clack-clackety, clack.

Toobit laughed, and then clicked back.

The alien responded with more clicks, and then Toobit returned with more again.

When the clicking conversation ended, the president returned to his putting green. "Just do what you need to do," he said to Flash.

Flash sighed in relief. His heart was racing and his legs were like jelly. He nodded and mumbled, "Yes, sir, Mr. President."

"Yes, sir, Mr. President," Toobit mocked in his own exaggerated British accent.

Flash approached the alien lying in bed and pulled the covers down to reveal its face. He had already seen these creatures up close a number of times, but their hideousness still took him aback. "Just a drop of medicine for you, old chap."

The alien's eyes widened. He sniffed. He tried to sit up but Flash forced him down with a hand to the chest. With his other hand, he pulled the vial from his pocket.

"Dr. Philip Winslow, here to examine the patient," said someone in an authentic British accent.

Flash spun to find the real Dr. Winslow at the door. Then, he turned to Toobit, locking eyes with the president.

"Lambo?" the president snarled. "Get him!" he ordered the guards.

Flash slipped the vial into his coat pocket as the guards grabbed him and cuffed his hands behind his back.

Toobit stepped in front and sneered at the Republican. "What exactly did you think you were going to do?"

When Flash didn't respond, Winslow chimed in, "I believe he was going to kill the patient with an overdose of RuSH^{2}O. Check his pockets."

A guard dug into Flash's lab coat and pulled out the vial.

Flash glared at Winslow and then shook his head in disappointment.

"I'm sorry, Mr. Flash, but I am a doctor, not an executioner."

The president took the vial from the guard and dropped it on the floor. The carpet stopped it from breaking, but he stomped on it, digging and twisting his heel until the glass was crushed.

Flash stared hopelessly at the ground. It felt like an eternity as he watched the blue liquid that could have saved conservatism seep into the carpet.

Then, just behind him, he heard sniffing. He turned to find the alien leader sitting up in bed.

Flash knew there was only one thing to do.

Without hesitation, he leaned back until he felt the alien's grip on his head--and then the creature's mouth over his ear.

The sucking began.

In one ear, he heard that grotesque sucking sound. In the other, the president's cry: "No! Stop!"

The pain only lasted a second.

***

Hozay walked along the suburban street, which was crawling with zombies going from house to house in search of brains. He took a bite of an apple that he had picked from a tree a few blocks back. Its crunchiness delighted him, as did the juicy sweetness that dribbled down his chin.

A thought command came, but it was weak and difficult to understand. It faded quickly.

All around him, the zombies fell, lifeless, to the ground.

Then, a strange feeling washed over the alien. A feeling which was completely foreign. It was liberating. Freeing.

He wiped his chin and took another bite of the apple. As he savored the taste, he looked to the heavens and thanked God for the place he could finally call home.

*** THE END ***

Thank you for reading. I hope you enjoyed the story. If so, please take a moment to review this book and share it with your friends.

Thanks again,
R. K. Delka

www.twitter.com/rkdelka
www.facebook.com/rkdelka